For Kristina Granström, with love
– M M & B G

Copyright © 2007 by Good Books, Intercourse, PA 17534
International Standard Book Number: 978-1-56148-568-0; 1-56148-568-3 .

Library of Congress Catalog Card Number: 2006026163

Text copyright © Mick Manning 2007 • Illustrations copyright © Brita Granström 2007

Original edition published in English by Little Tiger Press,
an imprint of Magi Publications, London, England, 2007.

Printed in Singapore

Library of Congress Cataloging-in-Publication Data

Manning, Mick.
Cock-a-doodle-hooooooo! / Mick Manning ; Brita Granström.
p. cm.
Summary: When a tired, lonely owl finds shelter in a hen house during a storm,
he is awakened by a flock of bossy hens who try to force him to be a cockerel,
until he demonstrates what he can do for them.
ISBN-13: 978-1-56148-568-0 (hardcover)
[1. Owls--Fiction. 2. Chickens--Fiction. 3. Individuality--Fiction.]
I. Granström, Brita, ill. II. Title.
PZ7.M31562Coc 2007
[E]--dc22
2006026163

cock-a-doodle-hoooooooo!

Mick Manning   Brita Granström

Good Books

Intercourse, PA 17534

800/762-7171

www.GoodBooks.com

One stormy night, an owl walked into a farmyard. He was cold, lost and lonely, with no place to go, so he squeezed through a hole in a shed.

It was warm and cozy in there, and he fell fast asleep.

In the morning Owl woke to a nip and a pinch. He heard clucking and squawking. He was surrounded by bony feet and beady eyes.

He was in a hen house . . . .

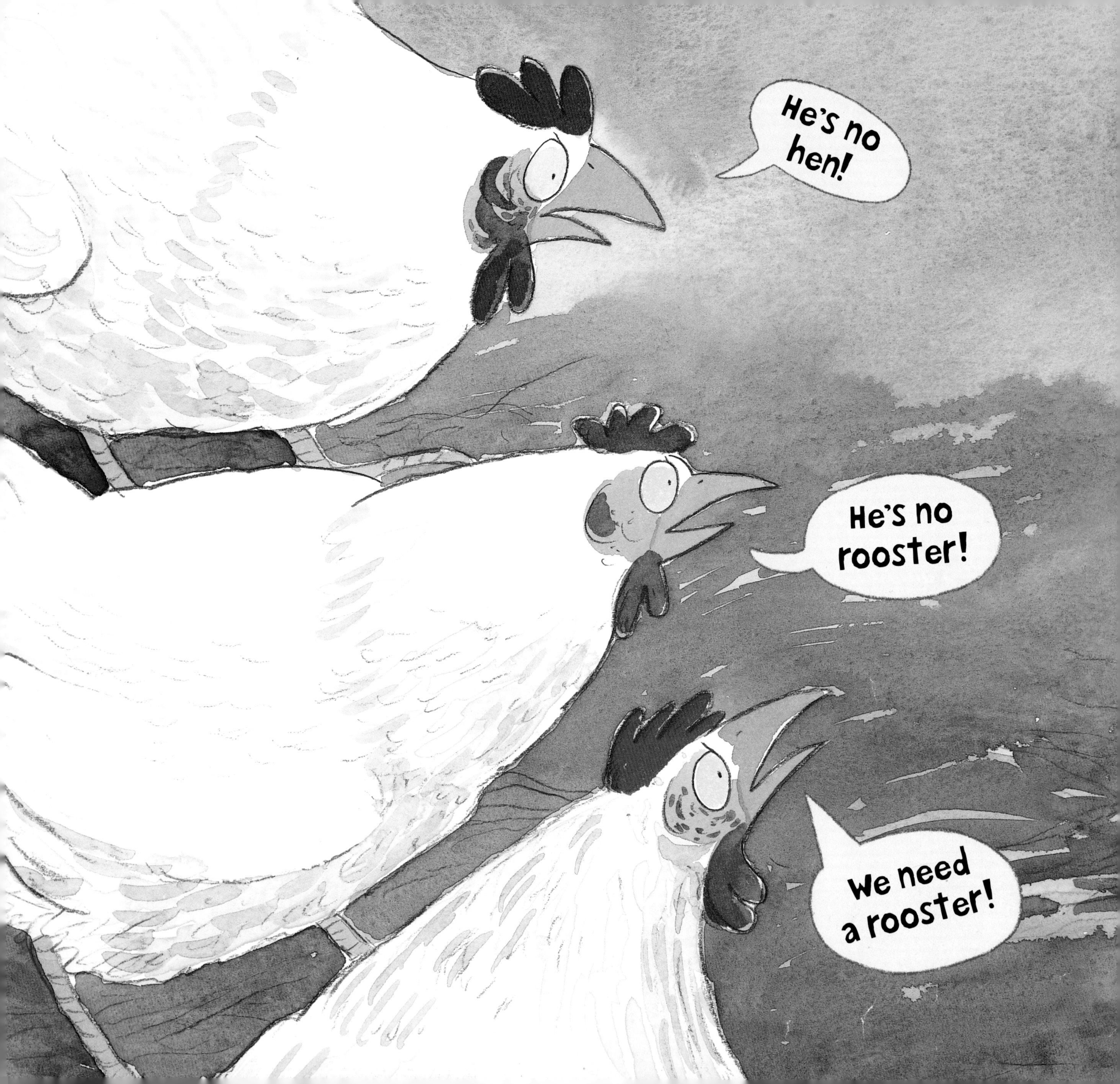
He's no hen!
He's no rooster!
We need a rooster!

"Can he peck like a rooster?"
said one bossy hen.
    Owl tried to peck.

"Can he scratch like
a rooster?"
    Owl tried to scratch.

"Can he cock-a-doodle
like a rooster?"
    Owl tried a cock-a-doodle.

HOoo!

The hens awarded him **NO POINTS** for pecking.

NO POINTS for scratching.

NO POINTS for cock-a-doodling.

"Hoo-hoo!" cried Owl sadly. He liked the warm, cozy hen house and the yard dappled with spring sunshine.

The speckled hen put her bony wings around him.

"I'll teach you how to be a rooster!" she clucked . . .

... and she did.
Owl learned how to ...

march up and down,

guard the hen house

and puff out his feathers!
He was doing very well . . .

... until the other hens said, "Try and cock-a-doodle!"
Owl tried very hard. He tried his best ...
but he was an owl after all,
and he just hooted like an owl.

Owl got cross. He'd had enough.
He was hungry and he was fed up
with the silly hens. So he said,

"I'm an owl, not a fowl!

Owls aren't hens.

We hoot in the moonlight.

We don't peck corn,

we catch . . . we catch . . . ."

"Rats!"

squawked a hen, peering into the
hen house.

The rat was stealing eggs,
eating corn, chasing chicks!

When Owl heard this,
he pricked up his ear tufts.
He flexed his sharp claws
and stretched his soft wings.
Then, silently as a floating
feather, he flew across
the hen house . . . .

Snip! Snap!

He caught the rat and gobbled
it up. The rat was tasty and
delicious. The hens were
speechless!

They fussed around
Owl in a flurry of
feathers and
clucks . . . .